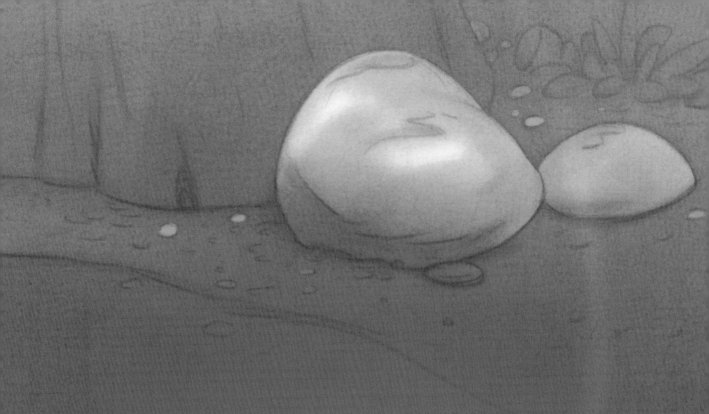

To my Grandma Faye and Grandad
Harry, who taught me that there is
magic to be found everywhere, if you
would only look.

MASCOT KIDS!

www.mascotbooks.com

A Fairy on My Sleeve

For more information, please contact:
Mascot Books
620 Herndon Parkway, Suite 320
Herndon, VA 20170
info@mascotbooks.com

Library of Congress Control Number: 2021908840

CPSIA Code: PRT0821A
ISBN-13: 978-1-64543-435-1

Printed in the United States

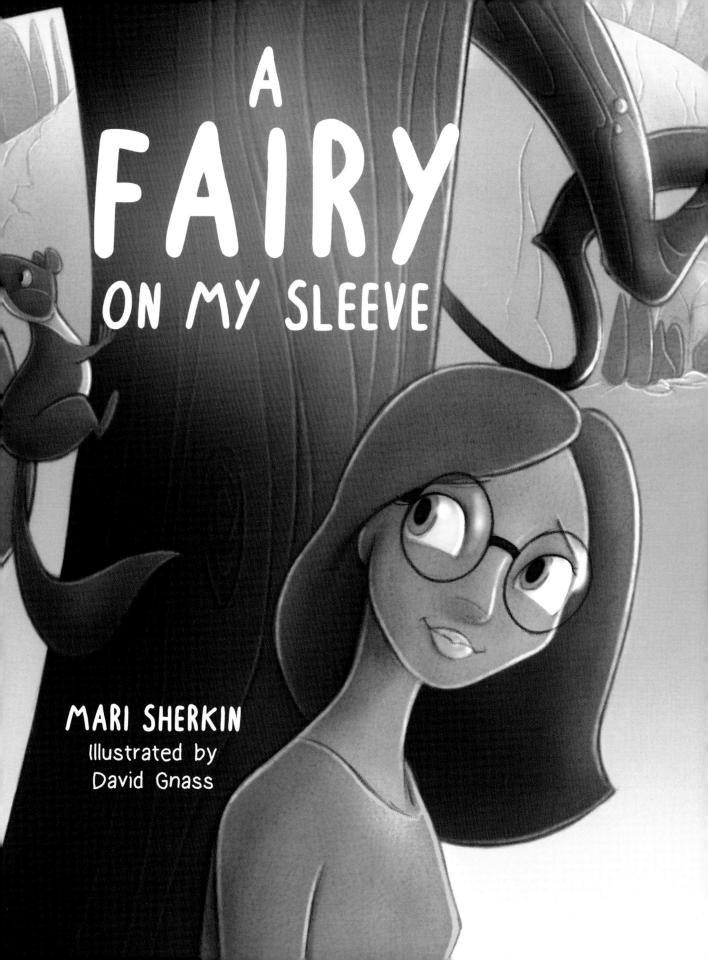

A FAIRY
ON MY SLEEVE

MARI SHERKIN

Illustrated by
David Gnass

If you look closely

through the

GREEN.

there are wonders to be seen:
that little glimmer in the sky
caught from the corner of your eye.

Look closer, there,
beyond that nook—

is that a fairy by the brook?

Flitting gently,
to and fro,

RISING HIGH

then skimming low.

Dainty and quick, wait, now she's gone.
They never seem to stay too long.
Which is why it's hard to believe
I had a fairy on my sleeve.

When I was small, I loved to read
of fairies, toadstools, stumps of trees—
so full of life, a happy place.
It put a smile upon my face.

It was a place to go and hide,
these gentle creatures by my side.

I always felt quite safe with them
in my make-believe haven.

"No more than tales," I told myself
about the stories on my shelf.
In fairies I could not believe,
but then one landed on my sleeve.

For way back then,
I hadn't seen
**the friendly
fairies of the
green.**

I did not know—but how could I?
I never saw them flying by.

I looked, of course, but did not see—
then one day it happened to me.
While I was reading under a tree,

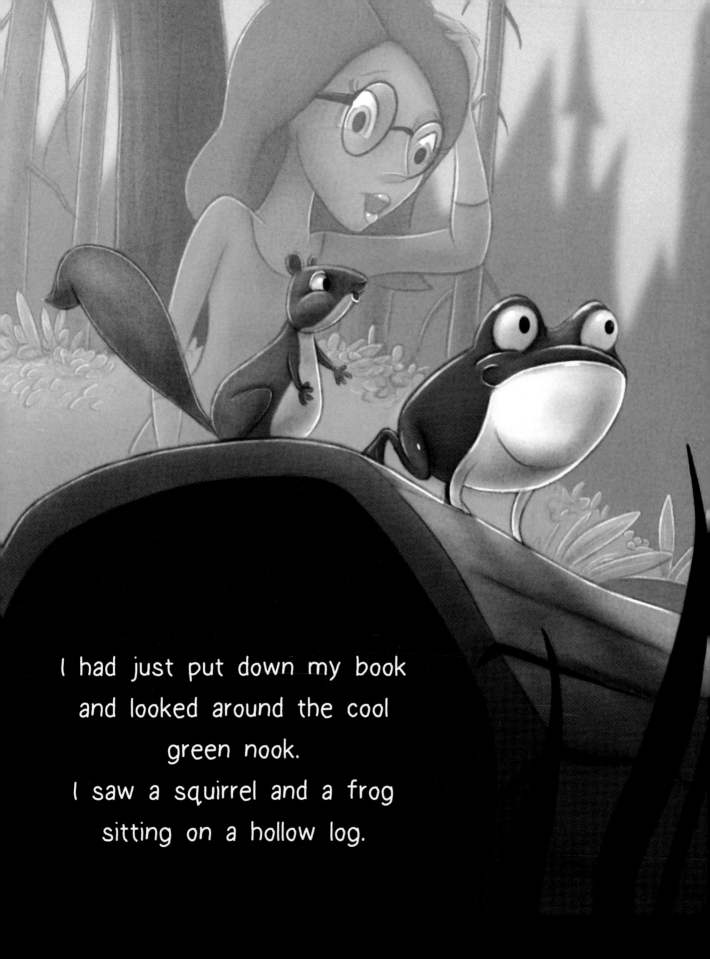

I had just put down my book
and looked around the cool
green nook.
I saw a squirrel and a frog
sitting on a hollow log.

Then suddenly, I saw
a light—
something had just taken
FLIGHT!

I held my breath and gripped my book,
almost too afraid to look.

But look I did, and what I saw
filled me completely up with awe.
Hovering before my face
was a fairy dressed in lace.

So delicate and beautiful,
translucent wings that
seemed to glow.
I was transfixed by her
sweet smile
and watched her for a little while.

"How can this be?"
I asked myself,
questioning my
mental health.

In fairies I could
not believe,
and then she landed on
MY SLEEVE.

She looked at me as if to see
what my reaction was to be.
I looked at her for quite a while
and gave her my most pleasant smile.

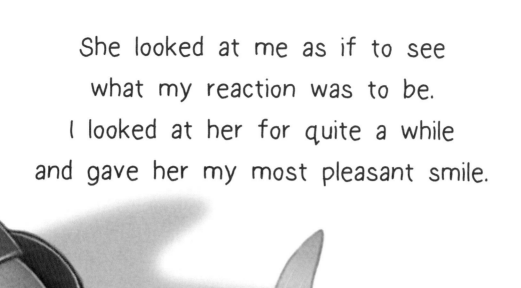

She smiled back and gave a nod,
then, quicker than a lightning rod,
**she flew straight up and
then was gone**

over the great
expanse of lawn.

I let out my breath and looked around
for any small sign on the ground
that she had been and I had seen

A REAL LIVE FAIRY

There was nothing for me to find.
No fairy dust was left behind.

No evidence, no little trail
**to prove my little
fairy tale.**

Now that I've told you and you've heard,
listen now and take my word.
Look closely, look
beyond the green, and

find the wonders

That little glimmer in
the sky,
caught from the
corner of your eye?

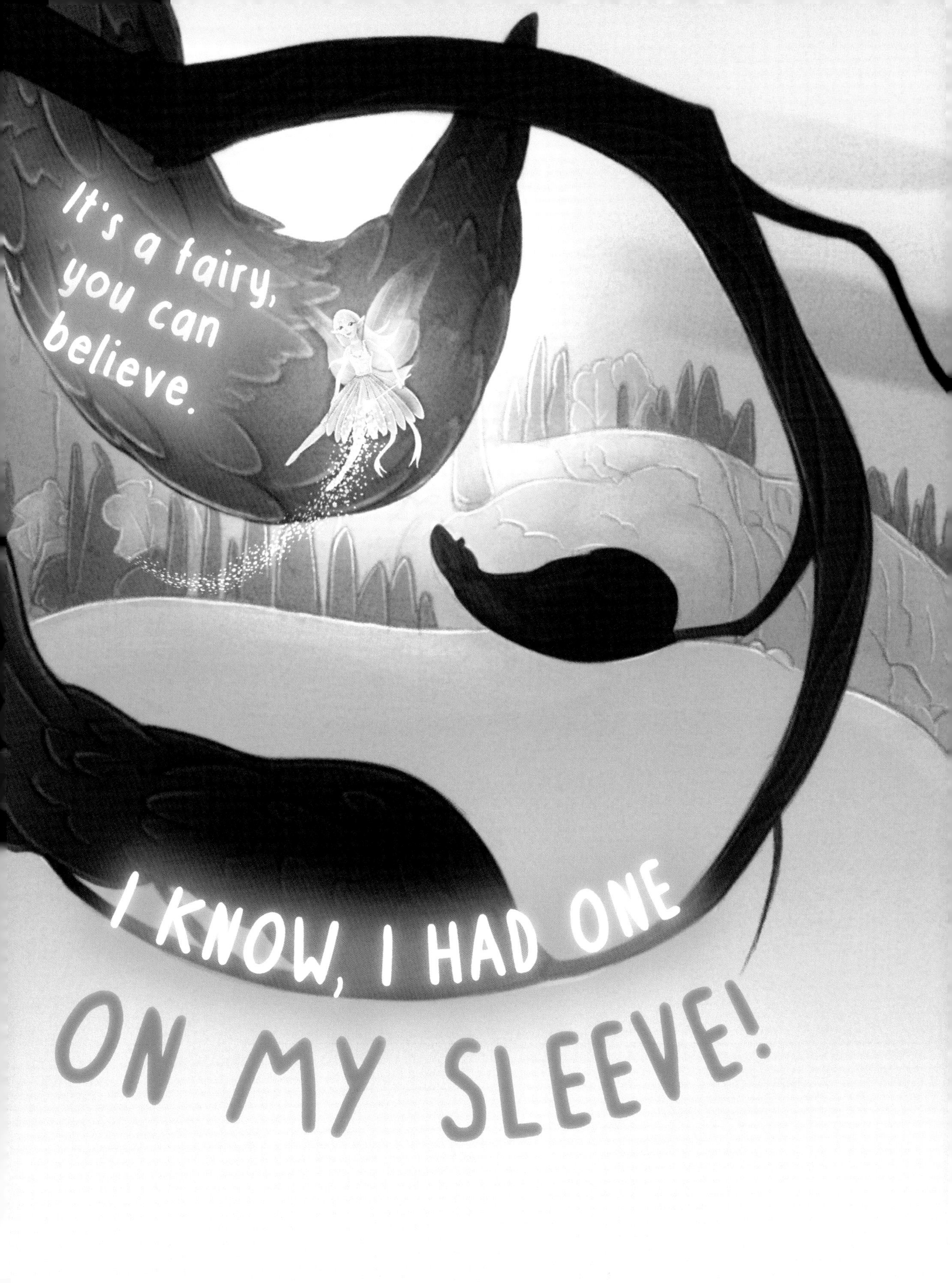
It's a fairy, you can believe.
I KNOW, I HAD ONE
ON MY SLEEVE!

About the Author

Born and raised in Toronto, Canada, to a British father and Canadian mother, Mari Sherkin spent many summers as a wee lass in England helping her Grandad in his garden while her Grandma read her fairy stories.

As an adult, Mari is still happiest playing outside in nature, be it the garden, the meadow, or the forest on her huge mountain property . . . and she still keeps an eye out for fairies.